**For Finn and Harper, who are each part Trixie,
part Professor von Junk, and always entertaining.**

IMPRINT
A part of Macmillan Publishing Group, LLC
120 Broadway, 25th floor, New York, NY 10271

ABOUT THIS BOOK
The art for this book was created with Adobe Illustrator and Photoshop. The text was set in Intelo.
The book was edited by John Morgan, art directed by Rebecca Kelly, and designed by Kevin Kelly.
The production was supervised by Raymond Ernesto Colón, and the production editor was Dawn Ryan.

Library of Congress Cataloging-in-Publication Data is available.
ISBN 978-1-250-19511-1 (hardcover)

Our books may be purchased in bulk for promotional, educational, or business use. Please contact your local bookseller or the
Macmillan Corporate and Premium Sales Department at (800) 221-7945 ext. 5442 or by email at MacmillanSpecialMarkets@macmillan.com.

Imprint logo designed by Amanda Spielman

First edition, 2019

10 9 8 7 6 5 4 3 2 1

mackids.com

Once, in a bookstore, a kid stole this book.
He thought he'd escaped with this book that he took,
but his fingers went numb and his eyeballs went smelly.
His skin turned the color of pumpkin pie jelly.
His face started swelling, his bottom was burning;
his festering nest of intestines was churning.
So, steal if you must, but remember this curse.
You'll envy that kid because you'll get it worse.

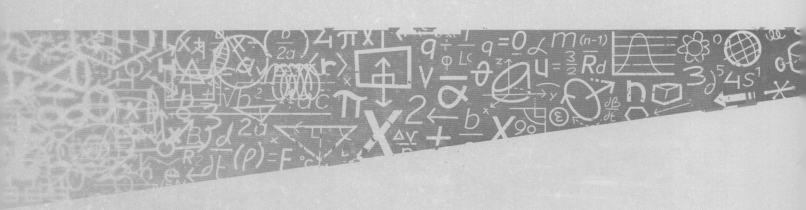

THE AWESOME IMPOSSIBLE UNSTOPPABLE Gadget

Kevin Kelly & Rebecca Kelly

{Imprint}
MAKE YOUR MARK

New York

The food isn't bad
and the campers are great.

And we get to take part in the famous tradition that's known as the

GADGETS GALORE
COMPETITION

There's one little kid here
with talent and spunk,
so we call him "Professor,"
Professor von Junk.

And he's got an idea for a gadget so clever
that everyone wants to help put it together.

So Newton

and Watson

and Babbage

and Bell

and Hubble

and Lovelace

and Morse

and Nobel

and Tycho

and Tesla

and all of the rest
gave up on their projects
to work on the "best."

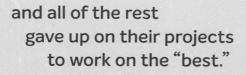

Everyone except me.

I think helping is nice, but I want to come up
with my own cool device.

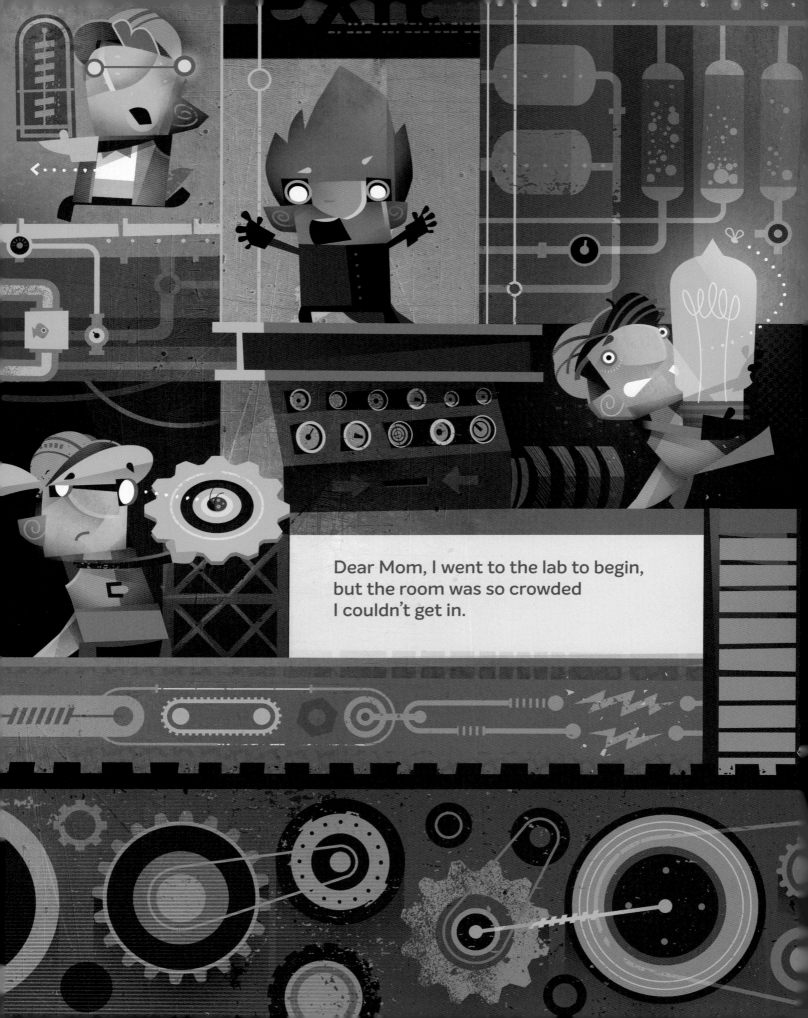

Dear Mom, I went to the lab to begin, but the room was so crowded I couldn't get in.

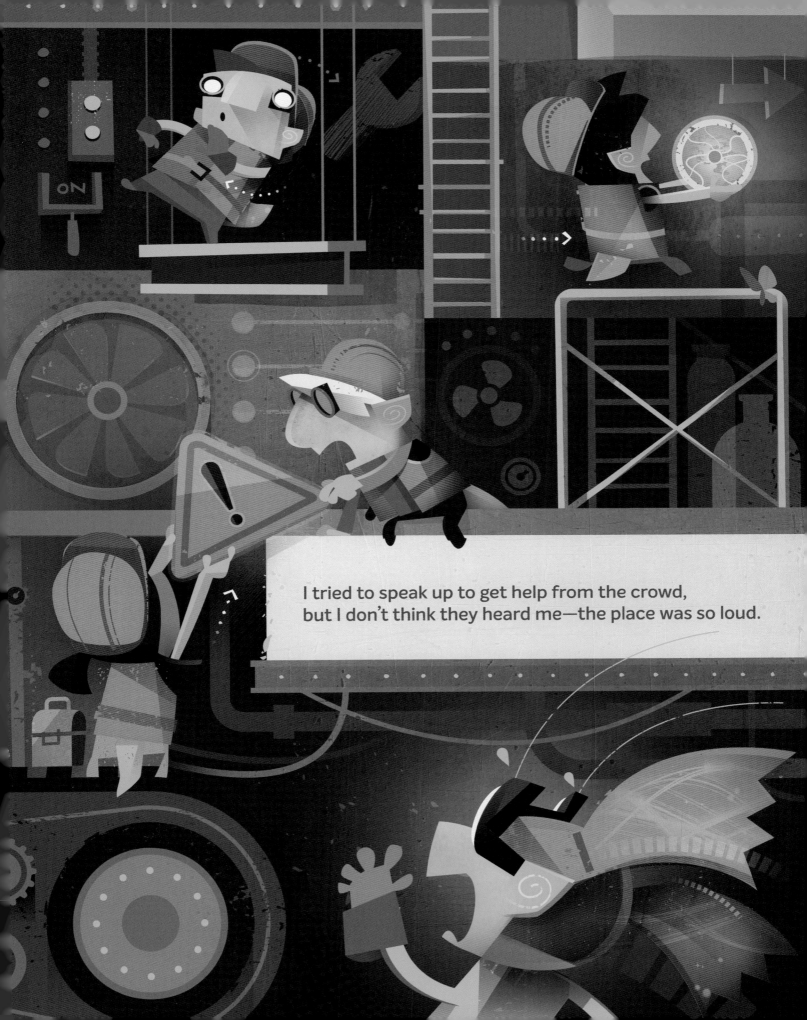

For a second I wanted to quit and go home.
But you're right—I can figure this out on my own.

A challenge was made. I refuse to refuse it.
What good is a brain if I choose not to use it?

Dear Mom,
I just realized
my cute little cabin's
the perfect location
to set up a lab in.

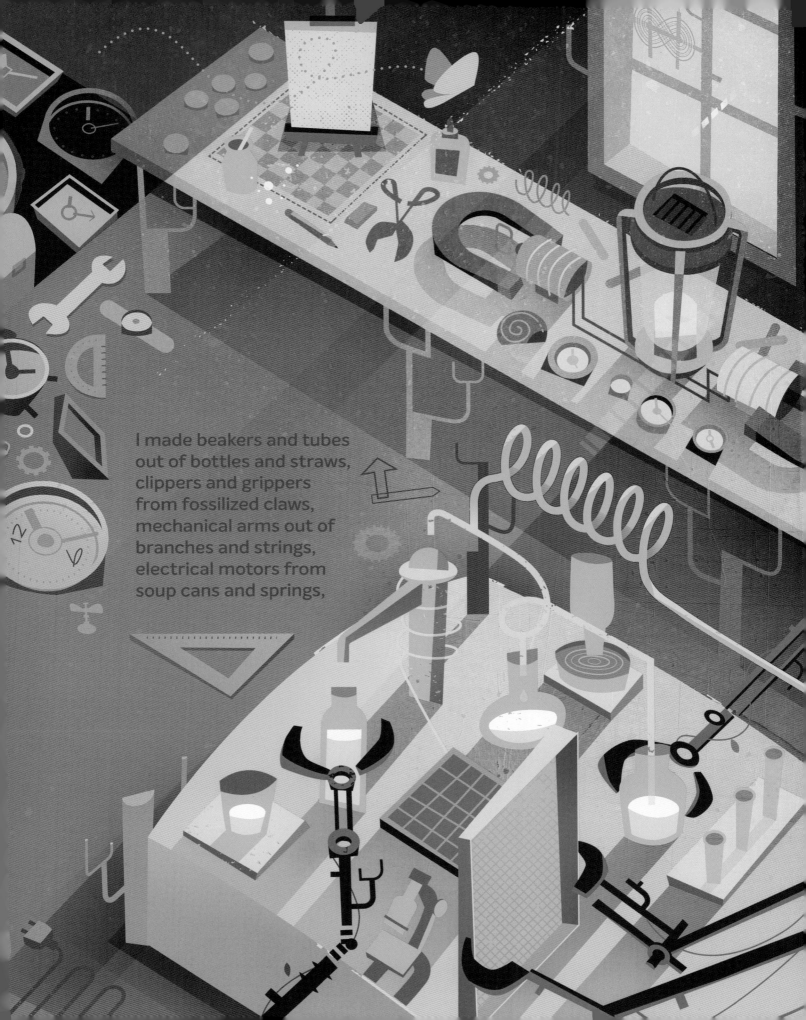

I made beakers and tubes out of bottles and straws, clippers and grippers from fossilized claws, mechanical arms out of branches and strings, electrical motors from soup cans and springs,

battery juice out of
sweaty old socks,
a dimensional
vortex from
magnets
and clocks.

And to give it
some sparkle once
everything's through—
dried macaroni and
glitter and glue.

Dear Mom, things have taken a turn for the worse.

My invention is working but runs in reverse!

So I went to the lab
for advice from the crew,
and I noticed a problem
with their gadget, too.

I tried making noises
and waving my arm,
but nobody noticed
my cries of alarm.

They continued to work on their wacky machine.

Professor von Junk was all over the scene, adding pipes and propellers and helium tanks and pistons and pulleys and cables and cranks.

And the more that they rushed
and the more that they hurried,
the more that they
missed their mistake.

I was worried.

INCREDIBLE
INVENTOR
PATENT PENDING

Dear Mom,
here's what happened:
von Junk and his team
were about to reveal
their enormous machine . . .

WELCOME TO THE ANNUAL

GADGETS GALORE

COMPETITION

Professor von Junk's INCREDIBLE

INVENTION INVENTOR

when they flipped on
the speakers and called
for attention.

" **Behold the invention
to end all inventions!** "

And before I had time to
convince him to stop,
Professor von Junk
pushed the button
on top.

Inventions,
contraptions, and
gadgets galore
came firing out
till they covered
the floor!

In less than a minute
the building was shaking
with things the
Invention Inventor
was making.

Everyone screamed and went running for cover
as gadgets, like magic, invented each other.

Gizmos and widgets were flooding the halls,
shaking and quaking and breaking down walls,
exploding like lava from gadget volcanoes,
and flying like Frisbees from gadget tornadoes.

And just as I thought, they had missed a small glitch.

It had an  button but not an  switch.

So I quickly pulled my gadget out of my pack, and raised it and gave my big button a *smack!*

TIME *Rewinder*

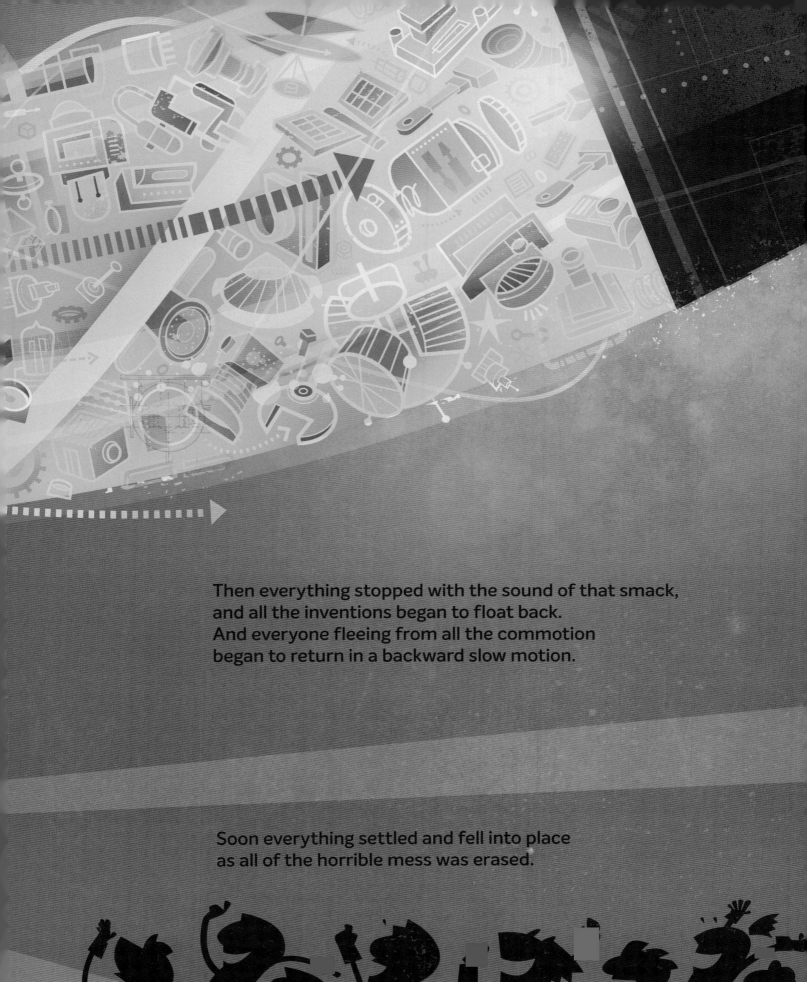

Then everything stopped with the sound of that smack,
and all the inventions began to float back.
And everyone fleeing from all the commotion
began to return in a backward slow motion.

Soon everything settled and fell into place
as all of the horrible mess was erased.

And you'll never believe it, Mom—
I was the champ!

And I got a new name
from the kids back at camp.
I can't wait to tell everybody
at school.

Kisses and hugs,

Professor
O'Toole